# A WHITE COLT'S TALE

# Saint Julian Press

## Story

# A WHITE COLT'S TALE

A Children's Christmas Story

Written By

Ron Starbuck

SAINT JULIAN PRESS
HOUSTON

Published by
SAINT JULIAN PRESS, Inc.
2053 Cortlandt, Suite 200
Houston, Texas 77008

www.saintjulianpress.com

Copyright © 2018
Two Thousand and Eighteen
© Ron Starbuck

ISBN-13: 978-1-7320542-4-0
ISBN-10: 1-7320542-4-X
Library of Congress Control Number: 2018914757

Art Images
Trinity Episcopal Church
Midtown Houston
Copyright © Saint Julian Press, Inc.

Author Photo Credit: Mary Beth Touchstone

TO THE PEOPLE OF TRINITY EPISCOPAL CHURCH
MIDTOWN HOUSTON

# CONTENTS

ANGELS WE HAVE HEARD ON HIGH ... 1

EMMANUEL ... 9

THE WISE MEN ... 15

ENTERING JERUSALEM ... 27

GOD IS SPIRIT ... 35

That they all may be one; as thou, Father, art in me, and I in thee, that they also may be one in us: that the world may believe that thou hast sent me. — John 17:21 King James Version (KJV)

# A WHITE COLT'S TALE

# ANGELS WE HAVE HEARD ON HIGH

# LUKE 1:26-33 (KJV)

[26] And in the sixth month the angel Gabriel was sent from God unto a city of Galilee, named Nazareth,

[27] To a virgin espoused to a man whose name was Joseph, of the house of David; and the virgin's name was Mary.

[28] And the angel came in unto her, and said, Hail, thou that art highly favoured, the Lord is with thee: blessed art thou among women.

# A WHITE COLT'S TALE

⁲⁹ And when she saw him, she was troubled at his saying, and cast in her mind what manner of salutation this should be.

³⁰ And the angel said unto her, Fear not, Mary: for thou hast found favour with God.

³¹ And, behold, thou shalt conceive in thy womb, and bring forth a son, and shalt call his name Jesus.

³² He shall be great, and shall be called the Son of the Highest: and the Lord God shall give unto him the throne of his father David:

³³ And he shall reign over the house of Jacob for ever; and of his kingdom there shall be no end.

*THERE* is always a story within a story, a tale within a tale. This is one of the myths told by the angels and archangels that watched over the Nativity the first night of Christmas.

A myth is a fairy tale that is truer than true, it is a story that grows stronger and stronger inside your heart as you mature in faith. A myth is a legend that inspires humanity.

It offers us a lesson in wisdom, as well as an inward change that brings our souls closer to God and creation. In truth, it is a story we know in our soul, one we have known forever and forgotten.

## 1 Corinthians 13:12 (NRSV)

[12] For now we see in a mirror, dimly, but then we will see face to face. Now I know only in part; then I will know fully, even as I have been fully known.

ON the same night, the Baby Jesus was born; a pure white colt was also born. The Holy Family gave him the Spanish name of Manuelo. This is Manuelo's story, and the

story of Jesus too. Jesus, whom the Prophets of Israel once told us, we would call Emmanuel, is God's gift of love to save the world.

This is still true even today, especially today, now in this moment. It is true yesterday too, as it will always be true tomorrow. And in all the yesterdays and tomorrows, we may try to imagine in a world without end.

# EMMANUEL

*EMMANUEL* means "God with us," and in Spanish so does the name Maunelo. So, Jesus and Manuelo, share a similar name with one another. Do you remember

these words from an Advent hymn we sing every year, VENI EMMANUEL?

> O come, O come, Emmanuel,
> and ransom captive Israel,
> that mourns in lonely exile here
> until the Son of God appear.
> Rejoice! Rejoice!
> Emmanuel shall come to thee, O Israel.

*AS GOD'S* special gift to the Baby Jesus, Manuelo was so happy to become his friend. You see, it was Manuelo's mother Isidora. Who wisely and humbly

carried Mary from Nazareth to Bethlehem. Where Mary gave birth to the Baby Jesus.

*ISIDORA'S* name means a gift of God in Spanish. The angels and archangels will tell you, that Isidora and Mary knew each other when Mary was first born. Manuelo and Jesus thought of this as God's magical circle of love. Do you believe in the magic of God's love?

# THE WISE MEN

*WHEN* the three wise men, who traveled from the East, came with their

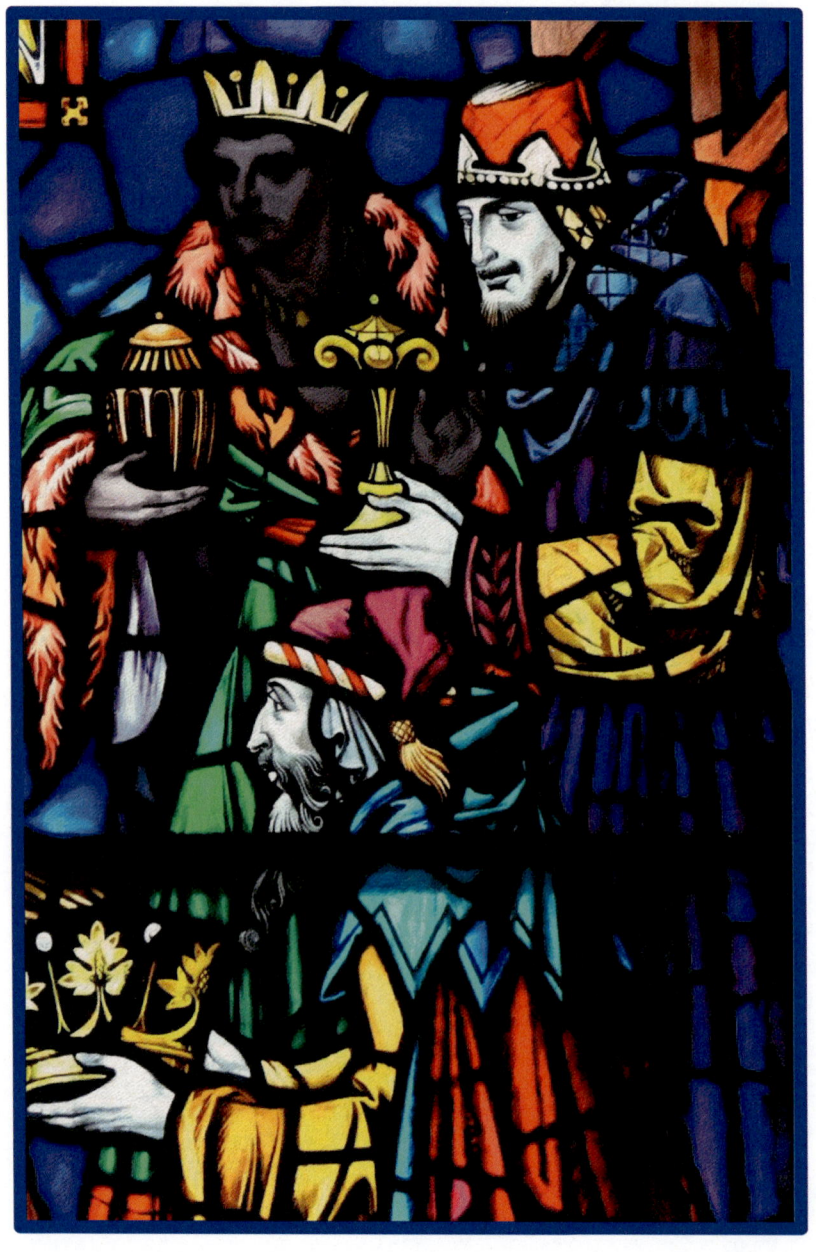

gifts of gold and frankincense and myrrh. They looked at Manuelo and Jesus and knew they would become best friends. Manuelo and Jesus were so happy to be with one another as extraordinary friends.

Manuelo and Jesus played with one other, ate with one another, and prayed with and for one another. Sometimes, they even fell asleep together like two innocent lambs. When Jesus as a young child started to school. Manuelo carried him from home to the schoolyard and back again.

*EVERY YEAR* at the feast of Passover, the family journeyed to Jerusalem to visit the Jewish Temple. On their journey, Manuelo carried Jesus across the Roman roads of Israel and through the ancient stone streets to the temple. Which is where Jesus entered our heavenly Father's house to learn and pray.

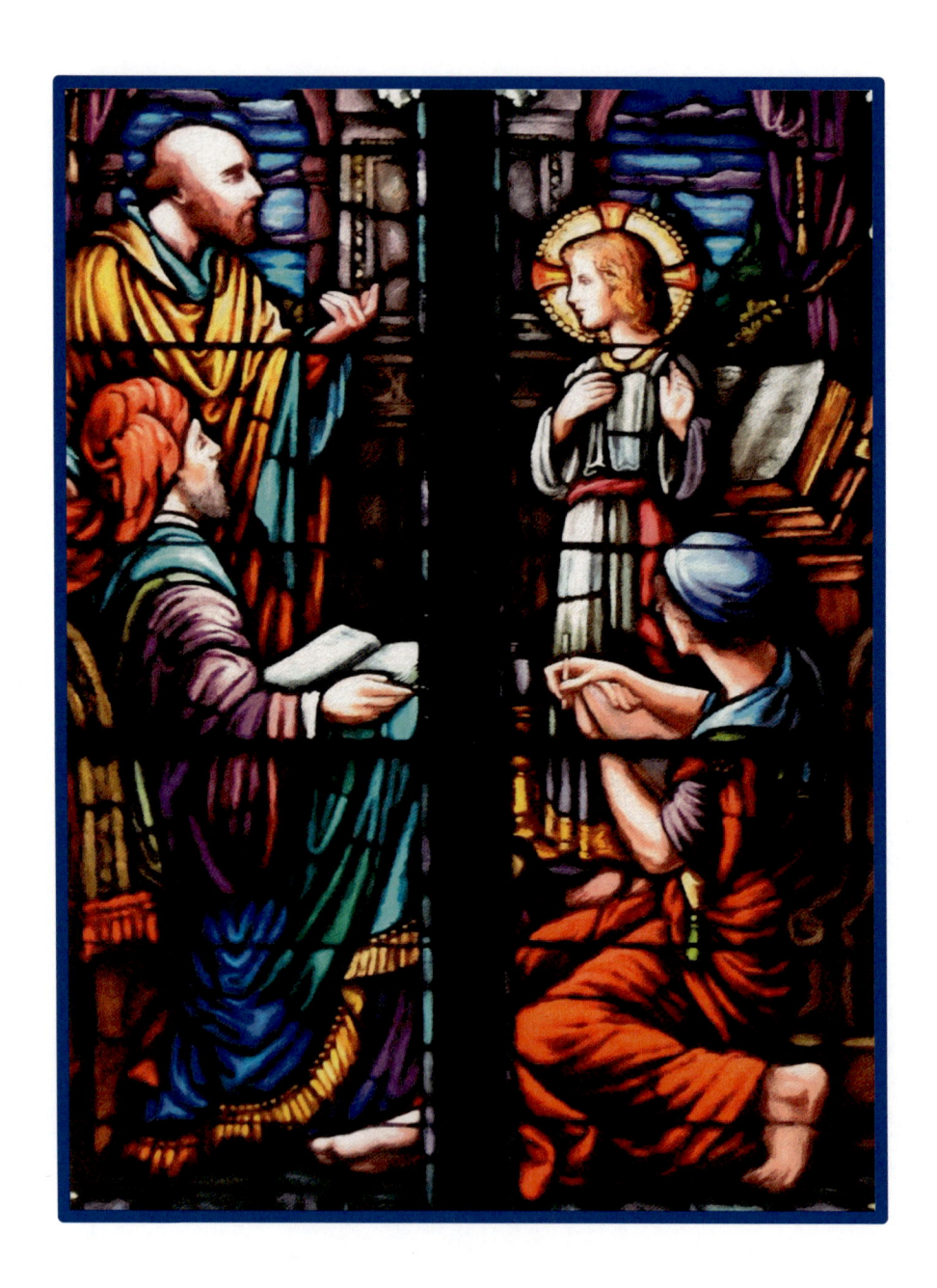

In the Jewish Temple, Jesus sat among the teachers, listening and asking them questions. They were all amazed at his inborn knowledge and understanding. Manuelo watched and listened as well and saw how Jesus grew in wisdom and stature.

*MANY YEARS* later, after Jesus was baptized in the Jordon River. When led by the Holy Spirit into the wilderness for forty days. Manuelo was there beside him, helping Jesus to make the journey.

*MANUELO* was there through all the years that Jesus lived. As Jesus ministered to the poor, healed the sick, visited people in prison, and loved everyone who was heartbroken or in pain.

*WHENEVER* Manuelo traveled with Jesus he told all the other animals they met about who Jesus was, and how he loved them. He explained to all who would listen how our father in heaven sent his only-begotten son into the world to save the whole world.

Everywhere they went together, children gathered, drawn towards Jesus, who loved them so dearly. And towards Manuelo as well, who they hugged and

petted and felt a special love for, as Manuelo loved them all.

"So we know and believe the love God has for us. God is love, and he who abides in love abides in God, and God abides in him." ~ 1 JOHN 4:16 (NRSV)

# ENTERING JERUSALEM

*WHEN* Jesus entered Jerusalem on what we now celebrate as Palm Sunday.

Manuelo holding his head high, carried him into the city. They were together before and after the Last Supper. When Jesus prayed all night in the Garden of Gethsemane, Manuelo prayed with him too. And on the darkest day of their lives, Manuelo was with Jesus. As Jesus beaten and crucified on a cross, committed his spirit unto to our heavenly father and died.

*WHEN* the Roman soldiers finally took Jesus down from the cross. Manuelo helped Joseph of Arimathea and carried Jesus one last time to his tomb. As any child can imagine, this was an extremely sad time for Manuelo, for he loved his friend Jesus so very much. And with every step Manuelo took, tears streamed from his sad eyes and fell to ground.

*AND* yet, Manuelo knew in some mysterious way. As our animal friends often know things we do not, that this was a part of God's plan to save the world. For as each teardrop touched the ground. Where Manuelo's hooves had carefully stepped, something wonderful happened. Each single tear turned into a beautiful priceless pearl. Which is a symbol of God's love for the whole world and the people in the world.

*For God so loved the world that He gave His only begotten Son, that whosoever believeth in Him should not perish, but have everlasting life.* ~ JOHN 3:16 (KJV)

IT is almost as if Jesus shared a secret with Manuelo. Telling him that he shouldn't be afraid and that they would see one another again soon. So, even though this was a time of great sadness for Manuelo, all his sorrow was balanced out by a great sense of joy. For Manuelo knew then, as he knows now that Jesus will always be with us. Even unto eternity and across all creation.

*AS* for Manuelo, his story continues up until today. He travels across all creation, always as an angel of light, telling his tale to all the animals and children he meets. You may see him appear sometimes as a Unicorn, a symbol of Christ. Jesus is forever a part of Manuelo, just like Jesus is forever a part of you too.

*JESUS* lives within us each and is with us ever now. The Holy Spirit dwells within us, praying in and with and through us. Especially, when we don't always know how to pray on our own.

# GOD IS SPIRIT

*Do not let your hearts be troubled, and do not let them be afraid.* ~ JOHN 14:1 (NRSV)

*God is a Spirit and they that worship Him must worship Him in spirit and in truth.* ~ JOHN 4:24 (KJV)

*That they all may be one; as thou, Father, art in me, and I in thee, that they also may be one in us: that the world may believe that thou hast sent me. ~ JOHN 17:21 (KJV)*

*But the Advocate, the Holy Spirit, whom the Father will send in my name, will teach you everything, and remind you of all that I have said to you. Peace I leave with you; my peace I give to you. I do not give to you as the world gives. Do not let your hearts be troubled, and do not let them be afraid. ~ JOHN 14:26-27 (NRSV)*

*Likewise the Spirit helps us in our weakness; for we do not know how to pray as we ought, but that very Spirit intercedes with sighs too deep for words. And God, who searches the heart, knows what is the mind of the Spirit, because the Spirit intercedes for the saints according to the will of God." - ROMANS 8:26-27 (NRSV)*

# MANY BLESSINGS

# &

# MERRY CHRISTMAS

# SAINT JULIAN PRESS

# ACKNOWLEDGMENTS

1. A special thank you to Trinity Episcopal Church Midtown Houston, for blessing the use of the stained-glass images for the book cover and interior art. All the artistic images used are from the main sanctuary of the church.
2. The interior art images were all created with a software program from the original digital photographs taken by the author, Ron Starbuck. Copyright © 2018 Saint Julian Press, Inc.
3. A history of Trinity Episcopal Church and details on all the stained-glass windows can be found in this book, **Pillar of Faith** – Trinity Church at 100 by Gayle Davies-Cooley. Copyright © 1992.
4. More information on all the stained-glass windows can be found in "Treasures of Trinity" – Plan of the Sanctuary and 100 Years of Memorial Giving, pages 137 through 176, *Pillar of Faith*.
5. The cover art image for *A White Colt's Tale*, was created from a photograph of the Unicorn in Captivity Window. In this image, entitled **The Unicorn in Captivity**, the unicorn is seen as the risen Christ in the Garden of Paradise. Page 171 – *Pillar of Faith*.

### INTERIOR ART IMAGES from TRINITY EPISCOPAL

1. Annunciation and Magnificat Window
2. Nativity and Epiphany Window – Angel above the Holy Family
3. Unicorn in Captivity Window
4. Nativity and Epiphany Window – Angel above the Wise Men
5. Nativity and Epiphany Window – Joseph, Mary, & Jesus Flee to Egypt
6. Nativity and Epiphany Window – Wise Men Offer Gifts
7. Nativity and Epiphany Window – The Holy Family under Guiding Star
8. Christ in the Temple Window
9. Sermon on the Mount Window
10. Central Africa Window
11. Australia Window
12. Hunt of the Unicorn Window
13. Christ in Gethsemane Window
14. Unicorn in Captivity Window
15. Christ Praying in the Garden of Gethsemane Window
16. Trinity Parish Window (Abstract Image)

# WORKS CITED & NOTES

**Angels We Have Heard on High**
1. LUKE 1:26-33 (KJV)
2. 1 CORINTHIANS 13:12 (NRSV)

**Emmanuel**
1. Veni Veni Emmanuel – O Come, O Come Emmanuel. 1861 Translation by John Mason Neale. Based on Matthew 1:23

**The Wise Men**
1. 1 JOHN 4:16 (NRSV)

**Entering Jerusalem**
1. JOHN 3:16 (KJV)

**God is Spirit**
1. JOHN 14:1 (NRSV)
2. JOHN 4:24 (KJV)
3. JOHN 17:21 (KJV)
4. JOHN 14:26-27 (NRSV)
5. ROMANS 8:26-27 (NRSV)

***Pillar of Faith** – Trinity Church at 100* by Gayle Davies-Cooley. Copyright © 1992. Published by Trinity Episcopal Church. ISBN: 0-9634160-0-6. Library of Congress Catalog Number: 92-082537.

# ABOUT THE AUTHOR

RON STARBUCK is the Publisher/CEO/Editor of Saint Julian Press, a poet and writer, an Episcopalian, and author of *There Is Something About Being An Episcopalian*, *When Angels Are Born*, and *Wheels Turning Inward*, three rich collections of poetry, following a poet's mythic and spiritual journey that crosses easily onto the paths of many contemplative traditions.

He has been deeply engaged in an Interfaith-Buddhist-Christian dialogue for many years, and holds a lifelong interest in literature, poetry, Christian mysticism, comparative literature and religion, theology, and various forms of contemplative practice.

He has been a contributing writer for *Parabola Magazine*. And has had poems and essays published in *Tiferet: A Journal of Spiritual Literature*, an interview and poem in *The Criterion: An Online International Journal in English*, *The Enchanting Verses Literary Review*, *ONE* from MillerWords (Feb. 2016), and *Pirene's Fountain*, Volume 7 Issue 15, from Glass Lyre Press (Oct. 2014), and *Levure Littéraire* (France – 2017 & 2018). A collection of essays, poems, short stories, and audio recordings are available on the Saint Julian Press, Inc., website under Interconnections.

Forming an independent literary press to work with emerging and established writers and poets, and tendering new introductions to the world at large in the framework of an interfaith and cross-cultural literary dialogue has been a long-time dream. Ron is a former Vice President with JP Morgan Chase and a public sector information technology Executive Program Manager.

Various Typefaces Used:

TYPEFACE: PERPETUA TITLING MT – LIGHT
**TYPEFACE: BASKERVILLE -** Baskerville
TYPEFACE: GARAMOND – Garamond